SEP 2006

E+
Red

Redbank,
Tennant.
   Barbie and
the magic of
Pegasus

Dear Parent:

Congratulations! Your child is taking the first steps on an exciting journey. The destination? Independent reading!

STEP INTO READING® will help your child get there. The program offers five steps to reading success. Each step includes fun stories and colorful art. There are also Step into Reading Sticker Books, Step into Reading Math Readers, Step into Reading Write-In Readers, Step into Reading Phonics Readers, and Step into Reading Phonics First Steps! Boxed Sets—a complete literacy program with something for every child.

Learning to Read, Step by Step!

Ready to Read Preschool–Kindergarten
• big type and easy words • rhyme and rhythm • picture clues
For children who know the alphabet and are eager to begin reading.

Reading with Help Preschool–Grade 1
• basic vocabulary • short sentences • simple stories
For children who recognize familiar words and sound out new words with help.

Reading on Your Own Grades 1–3
• engaging characters • easy-to-follow plots • popular topics
For children who are ready to read on their own.

Reading Paragraphs Grades 2–3
• challenging vocabulary • short paragraphs • exciting stories
For newly independent readers who read simple sentences with confidence.

Ready for Chapters Grades 2–4
• chapters • longer paragraphs • full-color art
For children who want to take the plunge into chapter books but still like colorful pictures.

STEP INTO READING® is designed to give every child a successful reading experience. The grade levels are only guides. Children can progress through the steps at their own speed, developing confidence in their reading, no matter what their grade.

Remember, a lifetime love of reading starts with a single step!

Special thanks to Vicki Jaeger, Monica Lopez, Rob Hudnut, Shelley Dvi-Vardhana, Jesyca C. Durchin, Luke Carroll, Kelly Shin, Anita Lee, Sean Newton, Mike Douglas, Dave Gagnon, Derek Goodfellow, Teresa Johnston, and Walter P. Martishius

www.stepintoreading.com
www.barbie.com

Educators and librarians, for a variety of teaching tools, visit us at
www.randomhouse.com/teachers

Library of Congress Control Number: 2005927120
ISBN 0-375-83296-3 (trade) — ISBN 0-375-93296-8 (lib. bdg.)

Printed in the United States of America   First Edition   10 9 8 7 6 5 4 3 2 1

Barbie™ AND THE

MAGIC of PEGASUS

Adapted by Tennant Redbank

Based on the original screenplay
by Cliff Ruby & Elana Lesser

Random House New York

Princess Annika
loved to skate.

She met
a polar bear cub
at the skating pond.
She named her Shiver.

One day,
the evil wizard,
Wenlock, appeared.
He said Annika
must marry him.

"No!" said Annika.
Wenlock turned
her parents to stone!

Then a flying horse
swooped down.
They flew away!

The horse was
Annika's sister, Brietta.
She was
under a spell, too.

To stop Wenlock,
they had to make
the Wand of Light.
They needed Courage,
Hope, and Love.

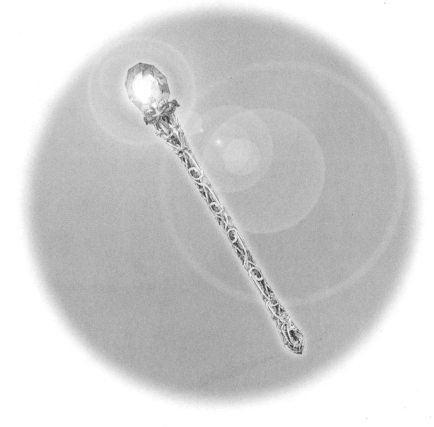

Brietta and Annika flew
to the Forbidden Forest.
They met a man
named Aidan.

There, a giant
trapped Annika.

She tricked him.

He put himself in chains.

Then she used a ribbon
as a rope.

Annika was free!

The ribbon changed
into a staff.

It was Courage
for the Wand of Light!

The friends flew
to an ice mountain.
They found writing:
Take only
what you need.

16

They found
a cave of diamonds!
Annika took one.
It was the Gem of Hope.

Shiver grabbed
lots of diamonds.
The ground shook.

The four friends flew

out of the cave.

They looked
for the Ring of Love.
It was Brietta's crown!

Aidan made

the Wand of Light.

The Wand's magic
wrapped around Brietta.
She was a girl again!

Wenlock found them.
Annika was mad.

"Destroy Wenlock!"
she told the Wand.
It didn't work!
Wenlock took the Wand.

The friends sneaked
into Wenlock's castle.
They found the Wand . . .
and Wenlock!

Annika grabbed
the Wand of Light.

This time,
she was not mad.
And it worked!

Soon after,
another spell broke.

Annika's parents
came back to life.

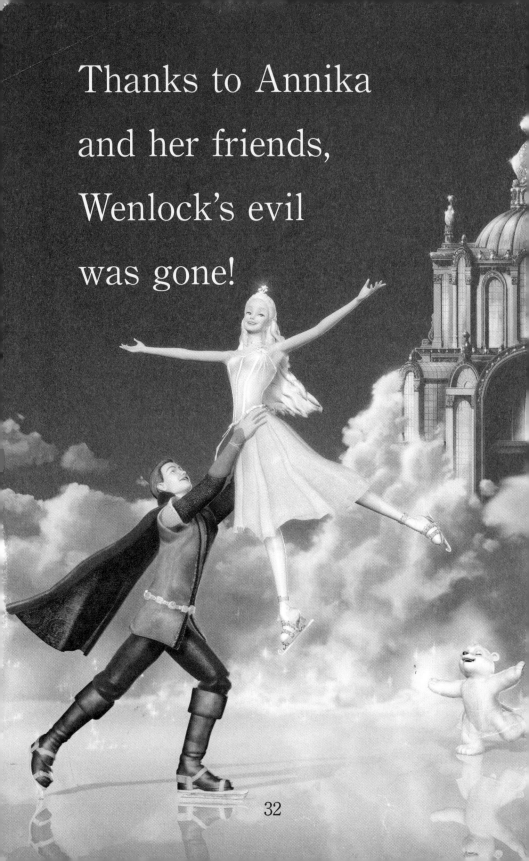

Thanks to Annika
and her friends,
Wenlock's evil
was gone!

32